Carmen and the Letter C

Alphabet Friends

by Cynthia Klingel and Robert B. Noyed

The Child's World®

The Child's World®

**Published in the United States of America
by The Child's World®**
P.O. Box 326
Chanhassen, MN 55317-0326
800-599-READ
www.childsworld.com

The Child's World®: Mary Berendes, Publishing Director

Editorial Directions, Inc.: E. Russell Primm, Editorial
Director; Emily Dolbear, Line Editor; Ruth Martin,
Editorial Assistant; Linda S. Koutris, Photo Researcher
and Selector

Photographs ©: Ryan McVey/Photodisc/Getty Images:
Cover & 12; Ric Ergenbright/Corbis: 11; Laura Bosco/
Corbis Sygma: 15; Chris Jones/Corbis: 16; Philip James
Corwin/Corbis: 19; Digital Vision/Getty Images: 20.

Library of Congress Cataloging-in-Publication Data
Klingel, Cynthia Fitterer.
  Carmen and the letter C / by Cynthia Klingel and
Robert B. Noyed.
    p. cm. — (Alphabet readers)
Summary: A simple story about a family visit to a cabin
introduces the letter "c".
  ISBN 1-59296-093-6 (Library Bound : alk. paper)
 [1. Country life—Fiction. 2. Family life—Fiction. 3.
Alphabet.] I. Noyed, Robert B. II. Title.
 PZ7.K6798Car 2003
 [Fic]—dc21   2003006620

Note to parents and educators:

The first skill children acquire before becoming successful readers is individual letter recognition. The Alphabet Friends series has been created with the needs of young learners in mind. Each engaging book begins by showing the difference between the capital letter and the lowercase letter. In each of the books on the vowels and the consonants c and g, children are introduced to the different sounds that the letter can make. Finally, children see that the letters can be found at the beginning of a word, in the middle of a word, and in most cases, at the end of a word.

Following the introduction, children meet their Alphabet Friends. The friend in each story encounters many words that include the featured letter of that book. Each noun that begins with the title letter is highlighted in red with the initial letter of the word in bold. Above the word is a rebus drawing that establishes a strong picture cue.

At the end of each book, we have included three words lists. Can your young learners find all the words in each book with the title letter in them?

Let's learn about the letter C.

The letter **C** can look like this: **C.**

The letter **C** can also look like this: **c.**

The letter c makes two different sounds.

One sound is the hard sound,

like in the word cat.

cat

The other sound is the soft sound,

like in the word city.

city

The letter c can be at the beginning of a word, like cow.

cow

The letter c can be in the middle of a word, like bicycle.

bicycle

The letter **c** can be at the
end of a word, like garlic.

garli**c**

My family and I like to come to the

cabin. The **c**abin is in the **c**ountry. It is

far from the **c**ity.

My **c**ousin **C**armen lives in the **c**abin.

She has curly hair. She is cute.

There are many trees near the **c**abin.

Carmen and I like to climb the trees.

Everyone climbs the trees!

There are **c**ows near the **c**abin.

A young **c**ow is called a **c**alf. The

cow and the **c**alf are hungry.

There are cornfields near the cabin.

Carmen likes to eat sweet corn from

the cornfield.

I love to come to the cabin in the

country. Maybe Carmen will come

to the city to see us!

Fun Facts

 A calf is a young cow. Usually, a dairy cow only gives birth to one calf at a time, but sometimes she has twins. A calf already weighs about 90 pounds (41 kg) when it is born. It can also walk just a few hours after birth.

 When you think of corn, you probably think of the corn you eat for dinner. But did you know that corn is also used to make plastics, paints, soaps, and to feed animals that you eat? Corn is so useful that the world produces about 660 million tons (660 million metric tons) of it a year. About 40 percent of the world's corn is grown in the United States.

 The cows in this story are dairy cows. That means that they are raised to produce milk. This milk is often used to make things we eat, like butter, cheese, and ice cream. But it can also be used to make some plastics, glues, and paints.

To Read More

About the Letter C
Klingel, Cynthia. *The Cabin: The Sound of* C. Chanhassen, Minn. The Child's World, 2000.

About Calves
Chase, Edith Newlin, and Barbara Reid (illustrator). *The New Baby Calf.* New York: Scholastic, 1984.

About Corn
Robson, Pam and Paul Robson. *Corn.* Danbury, Conn.: Children's Press, 1998.

About Cows
Doyle, Malachy and Angelo Rinaldi (illustrator). Cow. New York: Margaret K. McElderry Books, 2002.
Wood, Jackie, and Rog Bonner (illustrator). *Moo Moo Brown Cow.* San Diego, Calif.: Red Wagon Books, 1996.

Words with C

Words with C at the Beginning

cabin

calf

called

can

Carmen

cat

city

climb

climbs

come

corn

cornfield

cornfields

country

cousin

cow

cows

curly

cute

Words with C in the Middle

bicycle

Words with C at the End

garlic

About the Authors

Cynthia Klingel has worked as a high school English teacher and an elementary teacher. She is currently the curriculum director for a Minnesota school district. Cynthia Klingel lives with her family in Mankato, Minnesota.

Robert B. Noyed started his career as a newspaper reporter. Since then, he has worked in communications and public relations for a Minnesota school district for more than fourteen years. Robert B. Noyed lives with his family in Brooklyn Center, Minnesota.